Ding dong, ding dong!
Hip, hip, hooray!

There's someone
special here today...

Make some room;
let him get past.

The Entertainer's
here at last!

"Come in, come in!"
said Billy's mum.
"Tea?" Dad asked.
"Please, do have some."

"Your costume looks
so naturalistic!"
The Entertainer
grabbed a biscuit.

We must point out it's rather rude
to burp when someone gives you food.
I'm sure you know it's never right
to do a thing so impolite.

He scoffed the lot in one big slurp,
and thanked his hosts by saying,

"BURP!"

Mum looked quite shocked and said to Dad,
"His manners really are quite bad!"

The children chased him through the door,
where gifts were strewn across the floor.

(Among them, Billy's gift from Mum.) He stepped...

he slipped...

he whirled...

he **spun**.

"Wow!" they cried.
"This guy is fast!"

Then
CRASH!
his journey stopped at last.

It's always best, you know, I'm sure,
to pick your toys up from the floor.
The consequences, you'll agree,
of messiness are not pain-free.

The children clapped.
The children laughed.
"He is hilarious!" they gasped.

"Hilarious..." repeated Mum,
but thought, "I wish he'd never come!"

The Entertainer grabbed a jug
and drank the water,
glug, glug, glug.

Next, he took the flower bunch –
and chewed the stems up,
crunch, crunch, crunch.

And then the Entertainer found
a bowl of fruit. Mum looked and frowned.

Into his mouth, each piece he threw,
as Billy cried, "He juggles too!"

Down they went in one big bite.

"Bravo!"

the kids cried in delight.

"This guy is great!" they said to Mum.
"We're really, really glad he's come."

We advise you do not test
this hazardous way to digest.
Chewing helps release the flavour
and does your poor gut a favour.

When he'd finished
juggling fruit,
the children asked
to try his suit.

They tugged and yanked
and poked and ripped,
but couldn't find
where it unzipped.

BANG!

BANG!

He stopped the kids with big, brown paws (attached to which were long, sharp claws),

and reached out for a red balloon, when— BANG! he popped it.

The Entertainer turned and fled –
and found next door the birthday spread!

He licked his lips, his tummy rumbled.
Over to the feast he stumbled.

Never, ever help yourselves
to laid out feasts, or food on shelves.
It is polite, I'm sure you've heard,
to wait until it has been served.

The children found him in a heap,
snoring loudly, fast asleep.

"Oh no! The food!" gasped Billy's mum.
"It's in the Entertainer's tum!"

The children laughed, "You are a tease,
but can we have our tea now, please?"

Mum dashed to the refrigerator.
"What luck I saved the cake for later!"

They ate the cake.
It tasted splendid!
There the birthday
party ended.

Out the guests filed
through the door.
The Entertainer
waved his paw.

Billy said, "I'm so impressed.
That Entertainer was the best!"

He added, "Mum, can I be clear?
I'd like the same one every year."

Just then, the doorbell rang,

ding dong!

A man stood with a bear-suit on.

If a 'bear' turns up one morning,
hold him there and heed this warning.
Our advice could not be plainer:
check that he's your entertainer!

He said, "I'm sorry I'm so late –
I went to Number 28!"